P9-DFX-408

Peach & Blue

by Sarah S. Kilborne ~ paintings by Steve Johnson and Lou Fancher

Dragonfly Books™  Alfred A. Knopf ~ New York

DRAGONFLY BOOKS™ PUBLISHED BY ALFRED A. KNOPF, INC.

Published in the United States by Alfred A. Knopf, Inc., New York, and simultaneously in Canada by Random House of Canada Limited, Toronto. Distributed by Random House, Inc., New York.
Originally published in hardcover as a Borzoi Book by Alfred A. Knopf, Inc., in 1994.

http://www.randomhouse.com/

Library of Congress Cataloging-in-Publication Data
Kilborne, Sarah S.
Peach and Blue / by Sarah S. Kilborne ; illustrated by Lou Fancher and Steve Johnson.
p. cm.
Summary: A frog helps a peach see the world, and the peach shows the frog sights he has never seen before.
[1. Peach—Fiction. 2. Frogs—Fiction. 3. Friendship—Fiction.]
I. Fancher, Lou, ill. II. Johnson, Steve, 1960- ill. III. Title.
PZ7.K548Pe 1994 [E]—dc20 93-26562
ISBN 0-679-83929-1 (trade)
0-679-89095-5 (pbk.)

First Dragonfly Books™ edition: April 1998

Printed in Singapore
10 9 8 7 6 5 4 3

For my grandparents, P. & T.
– S. S. K.

One still summer afternoon, a large
blue-bellied toad wandered away from
his pond at the bottom of a small hill.
He jumped through the grass,
leaping high over the snake holes,
and climbed up and up and up
to the hilltop. There he rested
in the shade of a tree and looked
out over the pond below.

A raindrop fell on his head.

He searched the sky for heavy, stone-colored clouds,
but there were no clouds at all.

A few moments later, he felt another drop.
This time he looked directly above him into the tree,
and at the end of a thick, knobby branch
he saw a peach–with her eyes tightly shut.

More drops fell onto his head.

"Excuse me," called the toad.

The peach opened her eyes.

"I'm Blue," he said. "It's nice to meet you."

"I'm Peach," said the peach, surprised. "What are you doing here?"

"I came to see the view. Tell me, why are you crying?"

"The summer's almost over. That means I'm warm, round, and red from the sun, and I've grown all that I'll ever grow." Peach looked a moment into the tree. "This tree is my home, and I love my tree. But I wish I could see what the rest of the world is like. I want to feel grass, I want to touch animals, I want to lie down and look up at the stars. But I'm stuck to this branch and won't go anywhere until it's too late.... Soon I'll be picked and made into a cobbler or a tart, or eaten all at once by some stranger."

Blue shuddered.

"I wish I could walk," Peach said. "Then I'd walk right down this tree and into the fields. Is it nice by your pond?"

"It's all right," said Blue.

He told her about the moss and the ducks and the mosquitoes. He spoke of the leaves and the trees and the stone bench on one side. He described his brothers and sisters–all thirteen brothers and fifteen sisters.

Peach came from a large family too. She was related to all of the fruit on the tree. But none of the other peaches seemed interested in the world. Only Peach showed her face to the sun and the wind and the rain.

Blue walked around the base of the tree. He thought about tarts and cobblers, and wondered what they were. He thought about Peach being on the ground.

"I'm not scared to fall," she said.

A quick breeze suddenly caught Peach's branch. Blue watched her sway with the wind. She swung out high, came down low, swung back out high, and almost tipped off the branch.

"Stay there!" said Blue. "I have an idea!"

And he disappeared down the hill.

The next afternoon, Blue returned with his brothers and sisters. One by one, they jumped onto each other's backs, forming a tower. Blue sprang up last and landed directly beneath Peach. Then he stretched his arms around her, clasped her tightly, and pulled with all his might. *Snap!* Peach flew from the tree.

"Peach!" yelled Blue. "Wait!"

"I can't!" screamed Peach as she rolled down the hill.

Blue and his brothers and sisters leaped after her. The hill leveled out near the bottom, though, and Peach slowed to a stop on her own, right at the edge of the pond.

"Are you okay?" yelled Blue from high up the hill.

"Fine!" called Peach.

"Don't move!" warned Blue.

"I won't!" said Peach.

When they reached the pond, Blue's brothers scurried behind a stump and returned carrying a small bowl made of twigs and mud, with lily leaves on the bottom. Carefully, they lifted Peach and set her inside.

"We made this for you," they said.

Peach gingerly felt the mud, the lilies, and the twigs.

"Thank you," she said.

With a helpful shove from his sisters,
Blue pushed the bowl off the sticky, muddy bank
and onto the grass. There it glided easily.

"I will be your legs," said Blue, behind Peach.
"We'll walk wherever you want to go."

Peach opened her eyes wide.

"Oh my!" she exclaimed. "It's a harvest of colors!"

Blue looked at the damp old earth. "What do you see?"

Peach began,
"The green of the moss,
of the reeds, of the grass,
the red of my skin, of the ladybug's back,
the blue of your belly, of afternoon's sky,
the brown of the bank, of the eider duck's eye.
The white of the swans, of the kingfisher's eggs,
the cream of cocoons, of the whippoorwill's legs,
the silver of trout, of the damselfly's wings–
the beautiful colors of beautiful things!"

"You never told me about them!" said Peach.
"I never saw them before," said Blue.

They circled the pond the whole afternoon. They bumped over branches, slid down mud slips, bobbed in the reed bed. And Peach, all the while, discovered a pond that Blue had never seen.

When the sun began to fall, Blue set Peach gently into the water. He crawled onto a lily pad and tied the bowl to its flower. Together they watched the yellow and orange bows of the sun unfold over the fields. When all that was left was the moon, the two of them drifted in the dark, live night.

Shadows played off the pond. Crackling noises came from the bush. A bream leaped and–*splash!*–scattered waves and water over Peach and Blue.

"Would you like to sit on the bench for a spell?" Blue asked.

Peach nodded. Blue called to his friend the kingfisher and asked her if she could help lift Peach to the bench. In an instant, Peach was flying through the air.

"Th-th-thank you!" she said when she landed–bounce, bounce, bounce–on the stone. The kingfisher gave her a soft old feather to sit on.

"Pleasure's mine," said the bird. "But you rest up now. Seem a mite pale to me. Maybe need some *supper*." The kingfisher looked at Blue, then puffed out her chest and flew away.

Immediately, Blue scooped some water with a lily cup. He sprinkled a few drops over Peach and, even in the darkness, saw the color come back to her skin. She *had* been tired!

Next, he tore a branch from a willow, making sure that one end was dripping with tree milk, and gave this to Peach as he settled beside her. "It's not from a peach tree," he said. "But it's almost as good. Our willows are strong trees."

Peach smiled and sat up straighter. She rocked a bit with the night breeze, and Blue wrapped his arm around her so that she wouldn't slip away.

He looked at the great world about them. "You've shown me a special place," he said. Then he asked softly, "Do you miss your tree?"

"Yes," said Peach. "But I'm much happier now."

She relaxed in the crook of Blue's arm.

"I wish I could stay here awhile."

"You can stay here forever, if you like," said Blue. "I'd like you to."

"I don't think I'll last forever," said Peach.

"That's okay," said Blue. "Not many folks do. But until then, you have me, and I have you."